AGHA

the Eight-Mile Monster

AGHA

the Eight-Mile Monster

Karen Wilson-Timmons

ILLUSTRATIONS BY Marie Thérèse Dubois

INSIGHT KIDS
A MANDALA BOOK

San Rafael, California

Long ago, in a village called Vrindavan, young Krishna played with his cowherd friends. They took care of the cows and made up games. The boys acted out stories, dressed in flowers and leaves. For face paint they used river clay.

When they wanted to play tag, Krishna walked ahead. His friends ran to catch him.

"I'm going to catch Krishna first," one friend called out.

"Oh, no you won't," said another. "I will."

Krishna and his friends played ball with a lunch bag. They tossed it back and forth and tried not to break it.

When Krishna and his friends felt like running, they chased the shadows of birds. When they wanted to play music, they made flutes from river reeds and bugles from buffalo horns.

To cool themselves, Krishna and his friends swam in a river. They pretended to be frogs. When they were thirsty, they drew water from a well. The children hooted into the well and laughed at the echoes their voices made.

T he boys swung from trees like monkeys, danced like peacocks, and sang like cuckoo birds. "Cuckoo! Cuckoo!"

When they were with Krishna, his friends thought they could do anything.

One day a snake named Agha arrived in Vrindavan. Agha had magical powers, which he used to make mischief.

"These children think they are smart," Agha said to himself. "Let's see how smart they are. I'll swallow them."

Agha grew longer and longer until his body was eight miles long. He stretched his mouth wider and wider until it looked like a mountain cave. He unfurled his pink tongue, which ran through Vrindavan like a road. Agha sat there and didn't move. He didn't make a sound. He just waited.

The cowherd friends came singing and dancing down the road. They looked at Agha.

"That's not a cave," said one. "That's a snake pretending to be a cave."

"And this isn't a road," said another. "It's the snake's tongue."

"His breath smells like rotten fish," said a third friend. "I bet he wants to eat us."

"Let him try," said another friend. "Krishna will help."

The boys marched, unafraid, into Agha's giant mouth and waited for Krishna.

For a moment, Krishna didn't know what to do. "I must save my friends," he thought. "But how?" He followed them into Agha's giant mouth.

Heavenly beings, hiding in puffy clouds, cried out, "Krishna and his friends are in trouble. What will happen to them?"

Inside Agha, Krishna grew bigger and bigger. The giant snake choked on Krishna. His ugly eyes rolled around and around. Suddenly, his golden soul flew out of his body. It floated in the sky and wondered where to go.

Krishna found his friends unconscious in Agha's belly. His loving glance brought them all to life. Together they marched out of Agha's giant mouth.

When Krishna walked out of the snake, Agha's glittering soul entered Krishna's body and was at last at peace. Krishna blew his bugle and the boys gathered around him.

"What are we going to do with the body?" Krishna asked.

As usual, the boys knew just what to do.

Agha, the once-scary monster, became a wonderful eight-mile playground.

A NOTE TO PARENTS AND TEACHERS

AGHA THE EIGHT-MILE MONSTER is a retelling of an ancient Vedic tale that has been passed on for centuries in the oral tradition from parents to children. Many wisdom tales from India feature child Krishna and friends overcoming a monster or tyrant. Similar victories by youngsters appear in the works of Western author/illustrators such as Maurice Sendak, Mercer Mayer, and Wanda Gag. The satisfaction of young people finding creative ways to excel despite great odds and adversity affords a bridge that can lead readers to appreciate what might otherwise seem foreign in this age-old Sanskrit tale, retold from the Bhagavata Purana.

INSIGHT KIDS
A MANDALA BOOK

PO Box 3088
San Rafael, CA 94912
www.insighteditions.com

Text copyright © 2012 Karen Wilson-Timmons
Illustrations copyright © 2012 Marie Thérèse Dubois

Library of Congress Cataloging-in-Publication Data available.

ISBN: 978-1-60887-124-7

Design by Dagmar Trojanek

 ROOTS of PEACE    REPLANTED PAPER

Insight Editions, in association with Roots of Peace, will plant two trees for each tree used in the manufacturing of this book. Roots of Peace is an internationally renowned humanitarian organization dedicated to eradicating land mines worldwide and converting war-torn lands into productive farms and wildlife habitats. Together, we will plant two million fruit and nut trees in Afghanistan and provide farmers there with the skills and support necessary for sustainable land use.

Manufactured in China by Insight Editions

10 9 8 7 6 5 4 3 2 1